Hairy Maclary
from Donaldson's Dairy

Lynley Dodd

Spindlewood

Out of the gate
and off for a walk
went Hairy Maclary
from Donaldson's Dairy

and Hercules Morse
as big as a horse

with Hairy Maclary
from Donaldson's Dairy.

Bottomley Potts
covered in spots,
Hercules Morse
as big as a horse

and Hairy Maclary
from Donaldson's Dairy.

Muffin McLay
like a bundle of hay,
Bottomley Potts
covered in spots,
Hercules Morse
as big as a horse

and Hairy Maclary
from Donaldson's Dairy.

Bitzer Maloney
all skinny and bony,
Muffin McLay
like a bundle of hay,
Bottomley Potts
covered in spots,
Hercules Morse
as big as a horse

and Hairy Maclary
from Donaldson's Dairy.

Schnitzel von Krumm
with a very low tum,
Bitzer Maloney
all skinny and bony,
Muffin McLay
like a bundle of hay,
Bottomley Potts
covered in spots,
Hercules Morse
as big as a horse

and Hairy Maclary
from Donaldson's Dairy.

With tails in the air
they trotted on down
past the shops and the park
to the far end of town.
They sniffed at the smells
and they snooped at each door,
when suddenly,
out of the shadows
they
saw . . .

SCARFACE CLAW
the toughest Tom
in
town.

"EEEEEOWWWFFTZ!"
said Scarface Claw.

Off with a yowl
a wail and a howl,
a scatter of paws
and a clatter of claws,
went Schnitzel von Krumm
with a very low tum,
Bitzer Maloney
all skinny and bony,
Muffin McLay
like a bundle of hay,
Bottomley Potts
covered in spots,
Hercules Morse
as big as a horse

and Hairy Maclary
from Donaldson's Dairy,

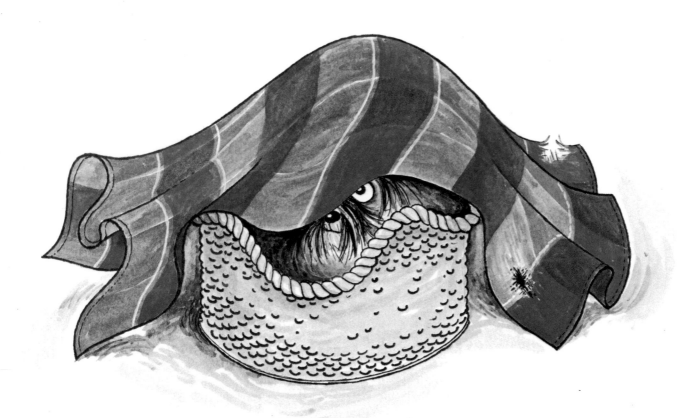

straight back home
to bed.

British Library Cataloguing in Publication Data
Dodd, Lynley
   Hairy Maclary from Donaldson's Dairy.
   1. Title
   823'.914[J]   PZ7

Other Lynley Dodd books

MY CAT LIKES TO HIDE IN BOXES (with Eve Sutton)
THE NICKLE NACKLE TREE
TITIMUS TRIM
THE APPLE TREE
THE SMALLEST TURTLE
HAIRY MACLARY'S BONE
HAIRY MACLARY SCATTERCAT
WAKE UP, BEAR
HAIRY MACLARY'S CATERWAUL CAPER
A DRAGON IN A WAGON
SLINKY MALINKI
FIND ME A TIGER

Published in 1983 by Spindlewood
70 Lynhurst Avenue, Barnstaple, Devon EX31 2HY.

First published in 1983 by
Mallinson Rendel Publishers Ltd.
Wellington, New Zealand.

Reprinted February 1984, February 1985, March 1986.
May 1987, August 1988, March 1990, May 1992
© Lynley Dodd, 1983

ISBN 0-907349-50-1

Typography by Bob Henderson.
Type set by Challis Datacom, Wellington, New Zealand.
Printed and bound by Colorcraft Ltd., Hong Kong.